FRONT COVER PHOTO: SWARNALI BANERJEE

Instagram: @the_creative_lens__

E Evincepub
Publishing

Evincepub Publishing

Parijat Extension, Bilaspur, Chhattisgarh 495001
First Published by Evincepub Publishing 2020
Copyright © Ishita Ganguly 2020
All Rights Reserved.

ISBN: 978-93-90362-31-8
Price: 299/-

STORIES FROM THE CITY CALLED KOLKATA

A COLLECTION OF SHORT STORIES

Ishita G.

'Guru kripa hi kevalam'

Dedicated to my Param Aradhya Gurudev, Mahamahopadhyaya Yogacharya Dr Ashoke Kumar Chatterjee, without whose blessings this book would not have been finished. Your light illuminated the path in my darkest hour.

ABOUT THE BOOK

"Stories from the City called Kolkata" is a collection of 10 short stories. Written in the backdrop of metro city Kolkata, the stories are based on urban middle-class life.

These are simple stories portraying love, joy, hope, heartache, and loneliness of city people – their struggles, frustrations, ambitions, and 'never say die' attitude. Each story has a unique plot twist, bound to melt the heart of the readers. The emotions expressed are relatable and the characters although fictional, are fleshed out of the real world.

The characters are mostly middle-class city people. A housewife who secretly writes poetries in a diary or a young office goer's fondness for an unknown woman on his daily commute, the good old gentleman Mr Bhaduri who struggles to maintain his huge mansion, the poor but virtuous rickshaw puller or Manotosh Babu who just wants to buy some cakes for his wife from an expensive cake shop or take the instance of the workaholic Riddhima who finally realizes the worth of life and finds true love at a ripe age – the characters are ordinary yet extraordinary in some way. They stand out in the crowd.

Each of the 10 stories has a message to give and a connection to make with the readers. This book is dedicated to the spirit of the Indian middle class city people and their zeal to survive and continue their life journey.

CONTENTS

THE DIARY

I t was the coldest day of December. Arundhati was drowsing on the couch. Lips half-open, chin resting on her right arm, her head dozed mildly to front and then back and then again to the front. The diary in which she was writing had fallen from her lap and was lying on the marble floor.

A thick band of sunlight entered through the open window and scattered over her feet. Arundhati was now in her fifties and looked plain enough with an odd mix of grey and dark hairs and dull skin.

If you had seen Arundhati in her youthful days, however, you would have been astonished by her beauty. Her facial features were perfect to such an extent that one would think she was a perfectly carved out pretty clay doll. To even intensify her doll-like looks, the Creator gave her deep brown curls and a petite attractive frame. Her voice, poise and intelligence were also perfect. In short,

Arundhati had it all. Her beauty was no match for anyone around her.

All girls of her age would secretly envy her. As if it was her fault that she was bestowed with such unparalleled beauty and quality. The other girls were not to be blamed either. The Creator seemed to have built them with less patience and not much care.

Well, not just beauty, Arundhati was a woman with multiple talents. She had a fine artistic taste. As a young girl she did sketches quite accurately even though she had never taken a drawing class. She also sang like an angel, but her best quality was unknown to even those who knew her. She penned beautiful poetries in her secret diary.

Maybe when you have it all you cannot get as much from life as you expect. The same thing happened with Arundhati.

She got married right after college to a man who was ordinary in every department possible. He was ordinary in appearance, in intelligence, as well as his behaviour.

Nobody remembered why she was married in such haste to such a plain man but back then people were shocked immensely. Her neighbours were curious, relatives were dumbfounded and friends were extremely unhappy to see such an extraordinary woman getting into the hands of such an ordinary man.

Initially, it was difficult for her to adjust to the new household. Her husband, Sujoy never took her out to the cinema or ever brought her a book let alone some flowers. Sujoy thought all forms of entertainment as a waste of money.

'We are middle-class people,' he would say. 'We shouldn't waste time or money on fanciful things!'

But Arundhati could not stop her likeliness for fanciful things. She grew beautiful flowers in abandoned pots and jars in her tiny balcony. Although she had forgotten how to hold a pencil for sketching, still, she got in art exhibitions with an armful of grocery shopping if she ever got a chance.

She cooked in the kitchen while listening to radio music. And in the lonely afternoons when Sujoy was at the office, she would pen down little poetries in a diary, nobody knew existed.

Although she never had a real-life romance in her lifetime, her poetries were all about love. She would feel embarrassed at times and also shocked at her audacity to write about love when she was a woman past fifty.

*S*he would then say to herself, *it's alright. This is the only outlet I have for my emotions. Let it be about love and fascination, heartbeats and fantasies!*

This afternoon she was reading from her diary. It was her most peaceful entertainment, reading those self-written poetries. She dozed off while reading and her diary dropped on the floor. The doorbell rang shrilly and Arundhati jumped.

It was Balaka, her neighbour. She sometimes came to visit Arundhati in the quiet afternoons to interrupt in her artistic pursuits. Balaka was a plump woman, chatty in nature and Arundhati's only friend in the apartment. Presently she entered the drawing room with a Tupperware in her hand and bringing fresh smell of caramel.

'Just made it! Brought some for you.' She handed the plastic box with a smiling face and settled herself on the couch.

'Why, there was no need dear! You always bring something or the other ...' Arundhati said fumbling with the box.

'You are my friend, aren't you? Can't I bring a little something for you, my dear?'

'Don't know how to thank you enough!' Arundhati smiled.

'Oh, it's just a little pudding, stop making a fuss! Keep it in the kitchen and come. I only get the afternoons free and that's when I come running to you.'

Arundhati went to her kitchen while Balaka absent-mindedly picked up the diary from the floor. Breathlessly she had half-read a poem from the diary when Arundhati entered. Her cheeks flushed, she stood there for a moment before snatching the diary from Balaka and then turned around.

Arundhati was overpowered by a strong emotion. She was feeling embarrassed for her secret diary being revealed and was guilty of the rudeness she had shown to her friend in snatching the diary from her hands.

But Balaka did not mind. She was a jovial woman who had seen many highs and lows in life. Although she didn't have an artistic bent of mind like Arundhati, she understood emotions more than anyone would expect her to understand and she observed and reflected on things nobody imagined her to be capable of.

The atmosphere of the room was almost as thick as her pudding, so, Balaka tried to break the silence.

'Why Arundhati, you never said you write such beautiful poetries?'

Arundhati got it all wrong. 'Go and tell everyone in your Ladies' club, then! I would be the great joke of the year! Serves me right, I guess!' Tears flooded her eyes and she was glad to have turned away. Staring at the wall she prayed Balaka would leave but she stayed quite at ease on her seat.

'What's wrong, even if I say, dear?' Balaka asked in a serious tone. 'And why would they laugh? Is writing poetries funny or is it so easy as making some pudding?'

Her words seemed to be kind and not hurtful. *Is Balaka seriously not making fun of me?* Arundhati thought.

'Come and sit here. And please wipe your tears.'

Arundhati did as was asked.

Now Balaka said in a seemingly enthusiastic voice, 'Why don't you publish your poems in a book?'

Now, this was all too much for Arundhati, though she observed her friend was saying these words with seriousness and pride.

'These are not that good!' said Arundhati in a low voice. 'Besides I'm too old!'

'What you're saying, my dear?' Balaka laughed heartily. 'These are excellent - I am serious! If you don't let anyone read them, how will you know if they're good or grand? And what did you just say - you are too old? Huh! You are what? 53? That's no age nowadays - plus what has age anything to do with creative pursuits?'

Her initial embarrassment having gone, the new prospect seemed to be quite frightening for Arundhati. 'But really—'

'Oh, you fuss too much! Let me talk with my husband. Okay? He knows about book publishing and all!'

Balaka's husband was an editor in a publishing house. Arundhati was now confirmed her friend was not joking with her. If she had promised to talk with her husband she had meant what she just said.

That evening Arundhati was smiling in spite of her. She cooked a nice dinner, dressed up carefully and also used the French perfume her daughter gifted ages ago.

Sujoy was surprised to see his wife in such great delight when he returned home. But he did not ask her anything. Arundhati also did not want to talk about the little discussion with Balaka that afternoon. She had never shown her diary to Sujoy. She thought of giving a little surprise to her husband. *When my book gets published I will gift him one!*

Somewhere deep inside, Arundhati was feeling a sense of accomplishment. She was a housewife for 33 years. Her college days seemed like a past-life to her. The colourful dreams of youth were now rusted and forgotten.

Today Balaka reminded Arundhati of her worth. So, at 53 she was still capable of doing something on her own. A book. Yes, her work is going to get published. She is about to become a poet to the world!

It was not money or fame that captivated her mind. As a young woman, she always wanted to become a renowned poet. But her dream got lost somewhere in the chaos and demands of life. Now she was unearthing a desire she had buried long ago.

'What happened?' Sujoy demanded at the dinner table.

'Why nothing!' protested Arundhati.

'You look quite unmindful and … odd ... if I might just say.'

'Oh, it's nothing! I was just thinking about Rinku.'

'Talking about Rinku, I just remembered! She called me up today. They are coming here for a month.'

'The last time we met Arko was a year and a half ago. How much he would have grown up?' Arundhati said fondly remembering the face of her ten-year-old grandson. 'I can't wait to see them!'

In the age of Skype and FaceTime, she lagged behind. Most of the conversations with her daughter and grandson were over the phone. The more they called her, the more she longed to meet them.

'So, when are they coming?'

'Next month!

'I have to make some preparations then.'

'Arko is coming! We can't let him play with dust and dirt,' said the excited grandfather. 'Clean the house, first. They live in such a clean country!'

The next few days Arundhati was engaged in cleaning and more cleaning. Not that she kept an untidy household but she had to make sure her home was comfortable and the very best for the home-coming Americans.

The walls were painted, mosquito repellants sprayed, old clothes given away, their daughter's room arranged and tidied. Arundhati mopped the stairs several times herself, removed old grease and stains from furniture.

The old house was shining quite brightly but Sujoy was still not satisfied. He critically observed every little detail, detected flaws and pointed out to his wife. She immediately started working on it. Arundhati worked day and night for the whole month till Sujoy could find no more flaws.

Just the day before their daughter would arrive Sujoy made a long list of items from sweets, chocolates, fruits and pastries to be brought from the stores to ingredients for foods to be cooked at home, doubly checked and then asked his wife to collect them from the market. 'I will bring the prawns and mutton while returning,' he added gleefully.

Arundhati hustled the entire morning. She did her chores, brought all the items and when it was afternoon she finally got some time to herself. She was thinking to sit with her diary when Balaka came. Her round-faced neighbour was panting in excitement.

'You know what? Your book is going to get published within a month or two! Give me that diary and rest my husband will take care of.'

'What? Seriously?' Arundhati shed a tear or two. 'I really don't know … how to thank you and Ajit da enough!'

'Oh please, it's nothing!' Balaka said happily. 'We'll want a treat from you though when your book comes out to the world! Now quickly bring that diary.'

'Yes, bringing it!' Arundhati rushed to her room. She opened her cupboard. But no - it wasn't there.

She searched all the racks and then the entire room. Where did she misplace the black diary? For years, she poured her heart into it. She never expected it to turn into a book but it was her solace - a small magical place where she could escape whenever she wanted.

Arundhati returned to the living room, her face pale as a ghost. 'It's not there … my diary! Don't know where it's gone!'

'What are you saying? It must be somewhere in your home!'

'I always keep it in the back of my cupboard. But it's not there!'

'Should I come along and search with you?'

'Please, come and see.'

For the next hour or two, the two women searched the diary in the whole house. But it was nowhere to be found.

Finally, when Balaka left, Arundhati sat quietly reflecting on life and why some people are always empty-handed how much they try.

When Sujoy came home he was aghast. 'Why is the house like that? I've put so much of effort to find on the last evening before my daughter arrives, the house been turned upside down!'

His wife did not reply.

'Arundhati, I am asking you something.' Sujoy's voice was rising now.

Arundhati, who was lost in her thoughts and obviously did not listen to any of her husband's words just looked at him now.

'What have you done with the house?'

'Oh, I was searching for something.'

'What did you have to search for rummaging the full house?'

'A black diary … an old one … quite thick, with golden borders on the top. Have you seen it?'

Sujoy was taken aback at this question. He thought for a while and then asked, 'Where did you keep it again?'

'In my cupboard … within a sandalwood box … the box is there but—'

'Oh, that one! Didn't I tell you that I've cleared the cupboard?'

'You have? Where have you placed my diary?'

'Well, you've done a complete mess in the cupboard - old newspapers, soiled books, diary and what not!' Sujoy said hotly. 'Sold all of those to the Kabadi wala last Sunday. He came in the early morning, you were sleeping then - I didn't want to wake you up. That diary was completely useless!

There was no address or phone number or anything important there, Arundhati! I've checked it before giving it to him. You could've asked me about it over the phone. Why would you have to create a mess?'

'You have sold my diary?' Arundhati said, her lips trembling and eyes becoming fuzzy.

'Yes, I said that already. Now can I get a cup of tea? And please, please clear all the mess you've done.'

Sujoy entered the bathroom muttering, 'What a clumsy woman!'

———❧———

WOMAN ON THE METRO

She was a pale-complexioned, medium-height woman. Almost all her features were ordinary but her eyes. Her dark black eyes had the capacity to take you to a different world or stop this one completely. It was not just her eyes were taken out of an artist's sketch book - her eyes were deep and magical. There was a kind of look in those eyes that will immediately attract you to her.

When she looked at someone they forgot the time and themselves. They wanted to know about her. It was not unusual, therefore, when her eyes met directly with Arpan's, his heart momentarily stopped. His mind captured that glance of her and he recollected it often or whenever he wanted, particularly in mundane days and sleepless nights. Arpan realized this woman had something uncommon in her, although what exactly it was, he was not sure.

Every morning this woman took the metro from Jatin Das Park and got down at Park Street. She would take out a book and read whether she got a seat or not. She was little older than Arpan, somewhere in her mid-20s. Every morning she entered the train from the same door and Arpan positioned himself such she would have to look at him even if she only gazed at him unmindfully.

Arpan was working in a small private firm at Esplanade and on the way to his office, it became more of a habit to watch this lady from the start to the end of her journey and then bid a farewell to her although in his mind.

She mostly wore light-coloured clothes, her dupatta hung carelessly from her slender body and her hairs always open, swung in rhythm with the train. Rarely, when she was not immersed in her book she would stand at the gate, eyes transfixed at some distance, lost in deep meditation.

Arpan often imagined in his mind of walking to her and asking something casual. He even got down after her on Park Street once. He wanted to introduce himself to her. Instead, he followed this woman, her dupatta had brushed his face - she did not notice him and he did not have the courage to talk with her.

He followed her till they reached a tall tower in Park Street - she must work in one of the hundreds of offices in that building Arpan had watched her enter from outside the gate. He stood there immobile, feeling the touch of her soft dupatta. He forgot the time. A push from a passerby brought him back to his senses but it was already late. When he entered office that day his boss shouted at him in front of everyone.

Today Arpan had come decidedly. He would get down at Park Street and on the platform would approach her. He even planned what to say so that he did not have to stutter on the first interaction.

It seemed the train was moving terribly slowly today. The gates closed later than usual at every station, thought Arpan. Rabindra Sarovar, Kalighat, and then finally Jatin Das Park - the gates opened and then closed. Where was she?

Arpan was travelling in this route for two years and this woman always entered from the same station through the same gate all these years. He commuted from Monday to Saturday and so was she. Arpan was regular and so was this woman. What happened to her today?

He was restless and in a bad mood all through the day. To make things worse, one of his colleagues annoyed him the whole day. So, when the day was over, he was quite pleased. His eyes inquired her among the rush and chatter of the returning crowd on the train.

For the full week, Arpan did not see that woman. He deduced a few theories. Maybe she was ill or someone else in her family was. Arpan prayed for her earnestly. Then the next theory hit him hard. What if she got a job somewhere else? Yes, this was possible. But how would he confirm on this? There was no way. Or was there?

Arpan went to the building at Park Street he had seen her enter a few months back. He did not know what to expect there. Somehow he thought of getting a clue.

He went to the main gate where a security woman sat at a desk with a register. A long line of people was signing in the register and hurriedly entering the building. Arpan watched and waited.

When the rush of the office goers was gone, he went directly to the security and said, 'Can you please help me? I work in a nearby office and I've come for some information.'

'About what?' the woman asked in a bored voice.

'Actually, it's about this lady I'd made an acquaintance with. She forgot her diary on the train - I just want to return it to her.' Arpan made up the story instantly.

'She works in this building? Which office? What's her name?'

'Yeah, she works here. But I don't know the other details. That's the problem, you see!'

'You don't know in which office she works?' the woman demanded raising her eyebrows. 'Not also her name?'

Arpan shook his head truthfully.

'In that case, I can't help you, Sir,' said the security woman flatly.

'I can give you her description. She is very fair and has these deep eyes. Her eyes are —'

'Look, I can't help you with this,' the security woman said impatiently. 'There are hundreds of people working here - can't know them all!'

Arpan sighed. He had come this far only to get dejected.

'One thing you can do though,' the woman added thoughtfully. 'Give me that diary and we'll put a notice on this desk so that whoever is the owner can claim it.'

'Er … no thanks, I'll prefer to give it to her … personally ...' Arpan replied. He turned to walk towards the gate.

A woman was entering through the gate who looked strangely familiar. She almost ran towards him smiling brightly. Arpan's heart skipped a beat. It was the woman from the metro.

Only there was something changed in her now.

Her eyes were now darkened with kajal. Her hairs were tied tightly in a bun. She was wearing a bright pink saree that matched the blush on her cheeks. A round maroon bindi on her forehead and a distinct touch of vermillion in the parting of her hair were blazing in the morning sunlight. She rushed like a cool breeze and passed Arpan for the desk - her aanchal blew in the air and brushed his forehead.

This was the last time Arpan met her - the woman with the dark black eyes that could take you to a different world or stop this one completely.

―――❦―――

LITTLE PIECES

OF SUNSHINE

I t was a dull day completely. And it seemed the weather wasn't keen on improving itself. The first half of the day was so hot that people could be seen walking on the streets completely soaked in sweat - shirts of gentlemen were glued to their protruded bellies and ladies were seen walking with cakes of powders deposited on their necks, moving in lethargy to do their errands.

Even the street dogs were so exhausted that instead of their usual enthusiastic strolls beside busy pedestrians, they were now curled up in shades, uninterested in the happenings of men and women.

When the scorching sun had sucked a lot of precious energy from the planet and was about to take a leave, it started to rain. It rained and rained. At first, people were delighted at its sight but when it didn't cease or slow down; everyone realized the day had been a complete waste. Children were stopped by their mothers from going outside and the evening walkers sipped tea lazily in the comfort of their homes.

On this evening when streets were lonely, doors and windows of houses were all shut tightly, a loud knock in old Bhowanipore interrupted the quietness of the lane.

A man was standing in front of a stained door of a mansion-like building. The house was ancient and quite keen on collapsing at any time. The walls were colourless, plaster falling off from places and the sound of a stereo was coming from insides of the building.

The incomer was wearing a pair of loose trousers and a worn-out sandal, his body was half-covered by a black umbrella as he waited for the door to open. A young woman opened the door quietly and allowed the man to step inside.

'There is no hope,' the man muttered more to himself.

The woman took the umbrella from her father. 'Why not Baba? This is our house! We have our rights …'

'Rights! What's that? You don't have any … at least where we live.' The man shook his head. He was in his mid-sixties, exhausted and dejected, burnt in the day and soaked in the evening. He moved slowly to his room while the daughter walked to the kitchen to make some tea, all the while feeling sorry for her old father.

This was their ancestral house. A few generations back the family was rolling in riches - their house was in full glory. Now the present owner had calculated money at hands and uncalculated troubles.

The tenants who occupied most portions of the building, like toxic weeds were damaging the house. The money offered to the landlord was a travesty of what he deserved because the rent was decided over a hundred years ago and not been changed since.

Mr Bhaduri returned from a court hearing today. His daughter and a few close friends insisted him to fight the case. Either he wanted a raise in the rents or an evacuation of the tenants. The court proceedings were moving in a snail-like fashion for over six years now.

He rested in his armchair; one of its arms had fallen away years back. The furniture in his room, although lacklustre now, was elegant, reminiscent of a foregone era when his forefathers were rich and extravagant. Portions of the ceiling were damped and damaged; neither he had the money nor the enthusiasm to do anything about it.

Mr Bhaduri had retired from work, seven years now. He was thin, feeble and a kind looking gentleman. Whatever energy and money he had, was getting wasted in the court proceedings whose results were doubtful to be in his favour. He knew the law protected the tenants and not the rightful owners of the land.

Mr Bhaduri wanted to take a nap. He was tired of the day and tired of life.

He closed his eyes and thought about life. Yes, he had covered a long phase of life, he had seen what he could see, had done what he could do - if he had to take a leave from this world now he was otherwise ready but for the sake of his daughter. *What is going to happen of her?* Ranjabati was 26 now, unmarried and doing an ordinary office job in a private firm.

It was past ten when the father and daughter finishing their dinner were about to go to bed when there was a knock at the door. It was still drizzling and besides who would come to them at this hour? They had almost no connection with the relatives and Mr Bhaduri's few friends and acquaintances were too old to come out in the rains just to meet him now.

The light bulb near the staircase was dead for a week and so the gentleman took a candle and went to answer the door.

'Oh, it's you!' It was Amlaan, their neighbour Mr Banerjee's son. 'Everything alright?'

'All good, thanks! Just had to ask you something – I'd seen you go out in the afternoon … wasn't sure if you'd returned … so I thought I'll come late!'

'That's alright! What is it, Amlaan?'

'Is it the right time to go inside and talk?' Amlaan asked hesitatingly. 'Otherwise, I'll come in the morning ...'

'Come on in … come on in!'

Mr Bhaduri took Amlaan to their drawing-room. 'Mind the steps, the lights out.'

'That must be giving you the trouble! I'll come and change the bulb tomorrow.'

'Oh, that would be very kind of you! I am not able to climb the ladder because of my arthritis —'

'You could've called me, Sir!' Amlan said in a dejected tone. 'I've told you already that any little help you need please don't hesitate to ask!'

'This old man didn't want to bother you!' Mr Bhaduri said cheerfully.

'Who is it, Baba?' Ranjabati came to see who the late visitor was. She and Amlaan were not friends nor were they in talking terms but they went to the same Primary school as children. And Ranjha's father was particularly affectionate towards this young man.

Amlaan started a business dumping college which failed. He had then started a second one. His parents and elder brother despised him for his fickleness. But Mr Bhaduri didn't know why he had a liking for this boy.

Amlaan was not like the usual young men. He had refuted the education system and wasn't even chasing a full-time job. He was experimenting with life. And what is life's worth without the experiments? Everyone was annoyed at him for his choices but secretly, didn't they all wanted to do something on their own at some point of their lives?

In their 50s and 60s, almost all middle class people repent on their choices and wish if only they had done something else when they were young – if only they could have taken some risk. And Amlaan was exactly doing that - taking risks, chasing his dreams. Mr Bhaduri was somewhat shocked and amused at his attitude towards life. All the same, he admired Amlaan.

'Sorry, I'd come this late,' said Amlaan awkwardly. He was answering Ranjhabati but looking at the blank wall behind her. Ranjha always found him strange.

Amlan now said to Mr Bhaduri, 'Sir, do you want to keep a paying guest?' Mr Bhaduri and her daughter exchanged glances.

'Frankly speaking,' Mr Bhaduri replied, 'I am fed up of my ancestor's choices in renting portions of this building. I don't want to add more trouble to my next generations!'

'But Sir, the person I am talking isn't the usual tenant … she is a young college girl who is searching for space and she is my sister's friend. Just give her one of your unused rooms.'

'There's a lot of space in here. But can't you see how our house is decaying? The tenants are paying peanuts and I don't have the capacity to maintain this property - I don't see how a girl would be interested to live in an unmaintained damped room!'

'That's not a problem as you think, Sir. The girl has come to the city for education. She just wants a shelter. Please agree, and the rest I'll take care of!'

Mr Bhaduri didn't know how to argue anymore with this persistent young man and had to agree. Although he couldn't see how a girl would be able to stay in his home. When Amlaan left, the rain had stopped and the roads were gleaming.

The next Sunday Amlaan came with his housemaid and a carpenter. They cleaned up the mess and did little repairs in an abandoned room of the house. Amlaan himself painted the walls and before night when the room was ready for the new occupant, the father and daughter were astonished by its appearance.

Even Ranjhabati had to appreciate Amlaan's skillfulness. She thanked him for the efforts. Amlaan did not reply to her. Ranjha understood that Amlaan was an odd person but she was grateful for the help he was doing to her father. They really needed the money and when the guest came the next morning and handed them a cheque of five thousand, Mr Bhaduri couldn't believe his eyes.

The next morning Ranjhabati met Amlaan on the way to her office. She always found him in a tiny tea-stall on her way, never showing any sign of recognition. Today she smiled at him and he stuttered a "good morning" when Ranjhabati had already reached the bus-stop.

*

Mr Bhaduri's arthritis became severe in the monsoon. He was down with a persistent fever. His daughter was trying all her best, doing everything the doctor had prescribed but her father wasn't recovering.

Ranjha took a leave for over a week and was on the verge of getting sacked. She was not worried about her job more than her dear old father. He was her only family and she never imagined how to exist without him. She had never seen her father complain in her life. Now he was whimpering in pain and lamenting all night. Her father would often have fits of unconsciousness. And then, he would mutter to himself completely unaware of his daughter's presence.

Ranjhabati was scared. With no friends to comfort and no hand of a relative on her shoulders, for the first time in life, she started feeling alone, afraid and helpless. She would stay in her father's room, morning and night, forgetting sleep and often food.

When she dozed off for a while, glimpses of a bitter reality haunted her in the dreams where she was fatherless and all alone in the big world.

One afternoon, a loud knock awakened Ranjhabati from a frightful fantasy. Her pained eyes felt at ease when she found Amlan standing at the doorsteps.

'I was just passing your house when I thought I'll just say a quick "hello".'

Ranjhabati started crying.

'What's happened?' Amlan asked worriedly. 'Is everything alright?'

With a sudden outburst of emotions, she clutched him and her tears drenched his shirt.

With a puzzled expression, he asked, 'Is your father alright? I haven't seen him for a week - please don't cry - and tell me what'd happened!'

Ranjha told him how her father was ill for days, unable to walk, uninterested to eat and sometimes even unaware of her presence.

Amlan went inside to see the old gentleman. He looked firmly at Ranjhabati and said in a determined voice, 'I'll handle this. Don't you worry - I'll not let him die.'

Ranjha, for the first time in these dark days, felt lighter. What with a friendly voice and an assurance, it seemed to her that the old, damped room of her father was now warm with a fresh ray of hope.

Amlan did what he promised. He called an ambulance and took the old gentleman to the hospital. He haunted the hospital, morning and evening. Mr Bhaduri was better in a few days.

When they brought him home, Ranjhabati was unable to find words to thank Amlan enough. Then she was also anxious about the hospital bills. She made a decision to sell from her mother's jewellery and repay her generous neighbour.

One morning when Mr Bhaduri was sipping tea with his young neighbour he asked him decisively, 'Amlan, I haven't asked you about the hospital bills. Please say how much was it and I will arrange the money in a day or two.'

'Sir, this is your time to take rest and heal. Don't you worry about that now!'

'Why not? I know that private hospitals are expensive! I won't let you bear the burden for me.'

'Please Sir, let's just forget it! If I were your son, would you think of repaying me?'

Mr Bhaduri fell silent for a moment and then said, 'My dear boy, you have done more than a son but I must repay your debts or I will not be at peace in this life or thereafter.'

'Sir, I can't take the money. I insist!'

Ranajhabati entered the room and joined in the discussion. 'I know my father. He will not rest until he repays you. You see, we are poor but we have self-respect... a good deal of!'

'But Ranjha ...' started Amlan.

'Please hear me out,' Ranjha said. 'We have a few empty, unused rooms and we know you have just started a business. Why not use one of our rooms for your work?'

Mr Bhaduri clapped his hands and supported his daughter gleefully. He was impressed by her intelligent decision. In that way, Amlan will not have to take the money which he was refusing and Mr Bhaduri could still repay his young friend.

The next morning Ranjhabati didn't see Amlan in the tiny stall on her way. While returning home in the evening, she found him standing alone, hitting a duce ball on a wall absently.

The awkwardness was now cast off between the two introverts. They have formed an inscrutable connection that never happened in their lives before. He was beside her when she was forgotten by the world. He had brought light in her dark days like a true friend. She was thankful to him but he didn't burden her with obligations.

'Amlan, what are you doing here?' Ranjha asked.

He turned at her and then smiled. His smile had the power to light up the world, thought Ranjhabati.

'Nothing, just nothing …' he said cheerfully.

'So, would you like to have dinner with us tonight? It's not much though … some chicken soup, rice and dal,' she added.

'If you are fixing dinner tonight it has to be delicious,' Amlaan said honestly.

'Haha … I must admit that I don't cook that well …'

Mr Bhaduri relaxing on his armchair watched two young people walking towards his house from the window. He remembered the day he was worried about his daughter sitting on this very chair. It was such a bad weather day and he was lost in miserable thoughts. And then there was the knock at the door late at night. Dark days had come and gone, with little patches of sunshine and moody rains. But it's alright now. There is someone up there who is watching us. Mr Bhaduri closed his eyes and smiled.

—~~—

THE

JEWELLERY BOX

T he jewellery dazzled as the fresh rays of sunlight entered through a corner window. This window was safe. It was in the quiet corner of the room. Nobody from outside was able to catch a glimpse of the lady or her treasure.

Subhra always closed her door when she checked on the jewellery. What happiness! Touching her pieces of jewellery she sensed paradise. Each of her golden friends was closer to her heart like no other being in the world. She closed her box, wrapped it in the old red linen and placed it safely in the vault.

She would sit with her jewellery box in the morning after waking up and at night before going to sleep. This was a daily routine she hardly missed. Subhra was aware her sister-in-laws laughed at her back because of this peculiar habit of hers.

At the age of 60, Subhra was not bothered about what others had to think or say about her. She had seen the good, bad and ugly streaks of life. People will always say something about you even if you are the sanest of the planet, still, they will dissect your character and have something bad to say about you. So, it didn't really matter to Subhra what her sister-in-laws thought about her.

She opened the door to find Meenakshi standing in front of her room. 'Do you want anything?' Subhra asked. She perfectly knew her sister-in-law was trying to sneak into the room and glimpse the contents of her jewellery box.

'Nothing Didi,' Meenakshi said in a falsely sweet tone. 'I'd come to ask you for breakfast ... will you like to have it now or later?'

Meenakshi was the wife of her second brother Abhinash. She was 50, dark, thin and nosy like hell - always interested in other people's lives more than herself. She had all information about the neighbours in her fingertips. She could tell you whose son had failed, whose wife just ran away or whose daughter got divorced.

And she loved to find faults of others. 'Mrs Chatterjee wore a red saree at the reception, can you imagine? In that complexion and that too at this age!'

'Sarvani lies so much! It was a fake and she kept telling everyone it was an original *Pochampally*!'

'Debjani's daughter won't get married or what? They keep telling she's pushing 30, but we all know she is passed 36 - what a waste!'

'I think Madhav Babu's son is a bit of a loser, what must he earn, not more than 8 or 10, I guess!'

She could go on for the whole day - analyzing others, finding faults, and entertaining herself by humiliating people at their back. Meenakshi always declared proudly to those who would listen to her, 'I'd the makings of a journalist! If only I haven't got married so early!'

Subhra quietly reflected that a journalist required more skills than being so meddlesome.

Subhra's other sister-in-law, Manoroma was the wife of her next brother Ardhendu. She was 52, extremely fair, robust in structure and almost resembled a marble pillar in a King's palace. Manorama was pretty in her youth and she continued to hold that belief. Frequent facials and layers of makeup could not hide the lines, age and conceit brought on her face.

Manorama, just like Snow White's stepmother thought she was the prettiest, fairest and most deserving of all women. Humans, particularly women were lesser mortals than her because they didn't have anything near to her. She had the perfect looks, perfect intelligence and of course loads and loads of money.

She was a proud woman, having inherited all her rich father's property, being the only child. Her husband was an Engineer and their only son a doctor - in short, she had it all! She privately admitted that nobody could actually pinpoint a flaw in her accomplishments so far. Manorama was self-obsessed and thought everyone merely existed to fill the planet while she was the chosen one to shine brightly among others.

Subhra came back to her father's house right after two years of marriage when her husband died. She was childless and returned home with a box containing all the jewellery her parents gifted her at the time of her wedding.

Her father and mother had passed away since and now she stayed in her father's house with her brothers and their families. She knew her brothers considered her somewhere between a responsibility and a burden and their wives tolerated her because they knew she had a box full of gold. People do care about gold than relations anyway.

She also knew why Meenakshi was nowadays giving her extra attention. She was always coming at her doorstep asking for breakfast or offering extra cups of tea. She was coming to her room every now and then, smiling unnecessarily and talking about things that didn't matter much to either of them.

Meenakshi's daughter, Jhimli was about to get married. The day has not yet been fixed but Meenakshi has already started impressing on Subhra so that she would offer some of her gold to her niece.

Yesterday only she said, 'Didi, the price of gold has increased so much … we won't be able to buy much for Jhimli! What can we do in this budget? You know your brother's income and … he has to take so many responsibilities! It's not just three of us, you know that …'

'Yes, you have to bear my expenses too.' Subhra had replied calmly. 'But I do have another brother and my expenses get shared, I believe?'

'Sure, it does! But Didi, don't mind, nowadays the price of things are all too much for middle-class people like us. We are not rich like Bor Da! Then there is always something or the other! Last month only, we had to pay one lakh for house repairs … I mean our share ... Bor Da managed the rest … but still one lakh rupees! I can't understand how my Jhimli will get all that she deserves. It's not her fault her father has to spend money on others …'

Subhra quietly smiled to herself. *Deserve.* What a word in the dictionary! Everyone thinks they deserve so much more but really does it matter even if you are the most deserving? If life decides you be empty-handed, you will remain so how much you claim that you deserve more.

Subhra was tired of these conversations. Either her younger sister-in-law talked about how pricey everything was or she tried to be extra sugary to her. Subhra very well understood the motive. She didn't say anything herself and waited for the question to be asked directly to her. And the question arrived at the dinner table that night.

Meenakshi passed a bowl of dal to Subhra and asked, 'So, Didi have you decided something for Jhimli?'

'Decide what?' Subhra replied.

Meenakshi exchanged meaningful glances with her husband before saying, 'You know your niece is getting married. So, what jewelleries will you give her? Have you decided anything?'

'Oh, when's her wedding? Is the date fixed?'

'Your brothers will go to her in-laws' house tomorrow and the date will be fixed - Didi, if you could tell us what you will gift her we could then decide on the remaining things! Weddings are expensive, you see, and we don't want to buy the same things for her. Like Bor Di said already she would give Jhimli a necklace set.' She pointed at Manorama unnecessarily with a sweet smile who returned the look of one who likes doing things for the less fortunate.

'Okay, then take Jhimli's share from me tonight,' Subhra said before leaving the dining table.

True to her words, Subhra took out a piece of fine jewellery from her box and handed it to Meenakshi in front of the others. It was a beautiful bracelet, peacock-designed, old yet looked so fashionable, the pride of young Subhra who last wore it in her husband's office party many years back. It seemed like a dream now. She remembered the night still. All eyes were on her - everyone praised the pretty young woman and her gorgeous peacock bracelet.

She was lost in thoughts when her sister-in-law brought her back to her senses.

'Didi, does it have a pair?'

'No, it is worn in one hand, that's the beauty of it!'

Meenakshi scorned. 'It's your only niece's wedding! Wouldn't it be nice if you gift her something heavy? … Something really impressive, you know.'

'Meenakshi, this bracelet is impressive and it's pure gold.'

'Yes, this is okay but you know what I mean! Could you not give something else with this then?'

'I can but give only this to her,' Subhra said softly.

Meenakshi now dropped her sugary tone and said, 'Really Didi, what will you do with so much gold? I thought you'll give something precious to my daughter.'

All eyes were on her but Subhra didn't reply back. Meenakshi glared at the bracelet and then at her sister-in-law.

Abhinash finally said it out loud what they might have been discussing at the back of Subhra. 'Didi, don't mind, but we really expected something more than just a bracelet from you!'

Manorama added, 'Seriously! You don't have a child. For whom are you saving all the gold?'

'This is all I could give. I am sorry.' Subhra turned and stood at her window.

Everyone left one by one but Subhra could hear whispered conversation outside her room. It was suffocating weather, cloudy, with a dark, star-less sky. Suddenly Subhra felt a soft pressure as Jhimli placed her head on her aunt's shoulder and embraced her from the back.

'Pishi Moni, I am really glad you gave me your bracelet - if you haven't given me anything still I would have loved you as I love you always!' Jhimli said slowly. 'Please don't mind what Maa just said.'

Subhra's eyes reddened. 'It's true, gold is what matters.' She breathed heavily. 'Gold is more important than relations, Maa was right!'

'What? Gold is more important than relations?' Abhinash and his wife had entered again.

'We can buy a bracelet for our daughter!' Abhinash blurted out. 'We have come to return your bracelet.'

'Didi, what were you were saying to Jhimli? We are after your gold?' Meenakshi turned to her husband, 'See for yourself what your sister was saying! We want her gold! And what about all that we do for her?'

'Maa! Please!' cried Jhimli.

'You keep out of this, Jhimli!' said Meenakshi angrily. 'Here, Didi take your bracelet! We don't need it! If you really don't have the heart to give, better don't give then!' Meenakshi thrust the bracelet into Subhra's hand.

Subhra's hand trembled. Ardhendu and Manorama were standing at the door. They were also saying something Subhra couldn't hear.

'I have something to tell you all,' said Subhra at last and all voices fell silent. 'It's a confession you might think. Those jewellery in my box are not gold.'

'What?' Remarked everyone at once except Jhimli, who looked as if she had a head cold.

'What do you mean?' said Ardhendu loudly from the door.

'Exactly what I said,' replied Subhra calmly.

'Impossible! Don't you lie to us! I know Baba had given you gold that's priced at least fifty lakhs in today's rate —'

'I'd once gone to a party with your Jamai Babu,' said Subhra. 'When we returned we found our house had been robbed - cash, clothes all stolen - my jewellery box lay open - all its contents gone. I was shocked and couldn't talk or eat or do anything for a few days. Those were not just gold for me but my parents' blessings.'

Subhra took a small breath and continued. 'Your Jamai Babu ordered all those ornaments for me again, the exact designs but these were now all in bronze, plated with gold. He promised me that slowly he would buy each of those pieces for me in gold. Till that time he said to keep the false ones with me or my parents, if they got to know would be hurt ...your Jamai Babu cared a lot about other people's feelings, you see. But within a few months of this incident, he had that accident and ...' Subhra's voice choked. Jhimli gripped her aunt with a pained expression.

'All your jewellery is false then?' asked Manorama coldly.

'Not all!' Subhra said. 'The ones I wore at that party were saved. My peacock bracelet, a necklace and the jhumka. I thought I will give the bracelet to Jhimli in her wedding and then the necklace later on as a post-wedding gift. And I have kept the pair of Jhumkas for my nephew's bride. Each of these pieces are solid gold, expensive yet priceless for me.'

'Didi, you could've said this earlier,' said Abhinash in a low voice.

'I told Maa after I came here. But she said to keep it to myself.'

'Why Pishi Moni?' asked Jhimli.

'Because she said my brothers and their wives will only look after me if they knew I had a box of gold.'

'Ridiculous!' cried Ardhendu.

'Yes, and it's true as I could see,' Jhimli sniffed.

Meenakshi was still not satisfied. 'So, why do you open your jewellery box every day? What is there to see if those are not gold?'

'I see something that you'll never understand,' said Subhra quietly.

—∼∼∼—

SULOCHONA'S

DECISION

Sulochona glanced at the house. It was a high-fenced large house adorned by a neat garden. No, the garden was not visible from the outside, only Sulochona had entered this house so many times that she knew what was in there. She knew each of the trees inside, the nooks and corners of the house and even its inmates or so she had thought.

The sky was darkening and the stars were coming out one by one - a cuckoo bird was calling desperately. Sulochona stood there for a while before turning away. She got a tuition job in this locality and this was her first day. When returning, the house stood in front of her at some distance and reminded her of the bygone days, unkept promises and failed hopes.

At first, she thought of refusing the offer. She never wanted to set foot in this locality again but the fee was too good for her to ignore. Sulochona Dey worked in a private school on a pitiful salary. This tuition was her opportunity to earn an extra thousand. Her student was quite obedient as she found out on the first day of the tuition. There was no reason to not continue the job. Besides she needed the money.

When she returned home her father asked as usual about the day and she had to tell that a colleague of hers had provided this tuition job after her school.

'Where is it, Tithi?' her father asked casually. Tithi was Sulochona's *daaknaam* or pet name. Bengalis usually have a different name at home to be called only by their parents and loved ones.

'In Lake Road area,' said Sulochona quietly.

Her father looked worried. 'Lake Road? Not near—'

'It's on a completely different side,' she lied quickly.

Sulochona was thirty-one years old. Her mother passed away when she was about seven. Her father had brought her up. He had retired ten years back from a clerical job. Money was always limited in this family but still, they managed to stay content with or without it.

Sulochona would have been in her husband's home by now. But life often does not happen the way we want. Her relationship of ten years was over last year. Her admirer of years said he did not love her anymore. And his parents, who knew Sulochona so well, hurriedly arranged and got their son married.

Sulochona deduced the reality of the situation later on. Maybe the man he loved so much had never cared for her. He was a doctor and while choosing a bride he very realistically chose one from his own profession. The world forgets to choose the ordinary. Love is forgotten and changed all the time and especially when a better prospect is found.

She was heartbroken at first but then she grasped the reality of life. You don't always get what you want - things don't turn out the way it should - and people you think you know can suddenly become strangers. Love often rusts in a pile of false hopes and faded memories.

In bed, she tossed and turned that night. People who left her kept walking in and out of her dreams. Her mother, her ex and a few other faces appeared and then faded away never talking to her.

The next day went as usual only Sulochona was a little unmindful. She did all her duties at school, even talked with the other teachers and smiled at students but it ached deep inside her chest.

*

The month of March was quite busy and uneventful for Sulochona. The usual school, tuition and chores at home gave her no time to rest or to complain. The thing she dreaded happened in April.

She was late from her pupil's home one evening and as she walked towards the bus-stop, she was face to face with a man and his wife who just got down their car. It was Shantanu, her lost love who stared at her and she at him – she paused momentarily and then walked away.

Sulochona's feet were heavy like they have been tied with iron chains. Still, she walked. Her eyes were hazy and the evening seemed to lack its colour. She did not hear the returning birds making uproar on the treetops. The world seemed to have lost its touch with her.

Sulochona remembered the last meeting with Shantanu. What did he say? Something about moving on. The words echoed in the insides of her head - magnified ten times. How she got up on the bus and how she returned to her home she never knew.

In her dreams that night she heard shrill voices and laughter, a man and a woman continuously laughing at her. 'You are but a loser,' the man said.

'Go away, leave me alone! Why don't you just leave me alone?'

'Tithi—'

'What?' Sulochona woke up with a start and saw her father standing beside her bed with a concerned look on his face.

'You are not well, Tithi, you didn't tell me,' he said gravely.

'I'm fine! I'll have to get ready for school.'

'The time is passed, dear. It's almost ten now … that's why I came to see if you are alright … and here you are down with fever …'

'Baba, I don't have a fever —'

'Yes, you have! I just touched your forehead, it's burning hot. And you were also saying things aloud … must be because of the fever, I must bring the thermometer and check - I just hope it's not that bad.'

Sulochona stayed at home all day taking paracetamols and feeling extremely weak. She stayed in her bed with a bad headache. Her father brought her food and time to time checked the temperature.

In the evening Sulochona started to feel better. A cool breeze entered through the open window along with the familiar voices of TV actors.

Sulochona checked her phone - no texts - no calls. She had no friends, her co-workers sent her texts sometimes but those were mostly related to work. She browsed an article on happiness. According to the writer, happiness is just a choice! The article said you can be happy if you want to be and you do not need the validation from someone to feel better. *Really, is it?*

Sulochona reflected on her life. She always sought happiness anywhere but from herself. *Decide to be happy, for happiness is a decision*. The article ended with this line.

*

The next morning Sulochona went out before her father woke up. She walked to the park to find a lady she made an acquaintance with, a year back.

There she was sitting on a corner bench; a book lay open on her lap.

'Good morning madam, do you remember me?' Sulochona asked the lady approaching her.

The woman looked up from her book and stared at her for a moment before responding, 'Yes, I believe we chatted a few times last summer.'

'Yes, we did! And you said you run a website for which you needed writers …'

'Sure. I did say that.'

'So, are you still looking for writers?'

'Well, yes, we always need some good write-ups.'

'Madam, you know what? I can write fairly well! Would you let me try?'

'Why not?' The lady smiled nodding approvingly.

Sulochona took the details in her phone, thanked the woman and returned home humming a song.

'Why Baba? Get up! I'm making your favourite alu parathas!'

Sulochona went to school and informed the Principal that she would leave the job in a month. All her colleagues were stunned at her sudden decision.

'Are you getting married?'

'Have you got a better job?'

Sulochona just smiled.

On the dinner table that night she informed the decision to her father.

'Are you sure? It was kind of a secure job.'

'Only I didn't really enjoy doing it! I've always wanted to pursue writing as a career.'

'Writing as a career? Are you sure? I don't think it's a —'

'It's all right Baba,' Sulochona said. 'I need to take a chance. Otherwise, how will I know what life has to offer me?'

'But …'

'Please Baba … I know I've made a lot of mistakes - taken a lot of bad decisions in life but I've never thought clearly about what I was doing then! But I am so sure about *this* … I just know I've what it takes to be a writer! And I got this one opportunity which I don't want to miss – I've to give it a try!'

'Okay! If you really want to do this I won't discourage you. What about the tuition at Lake Road? I think you should drop that one.'

'No, Baba. I've promised the child's parents that I'll help her out. The girl needs my guidance.'

'What if you meet Shantanu on the way?' Sulochona's father shook his head. 'I really don't want you to face him again in this life.'

'It's okay Baba. We've met.'

'What? Did he say anything to you?'

'What is there for him to say?' said Sulochona, clearing the plates. 'Besides he doesn't matter to me. Not anymore.'

THE QUESTION

P ushpendu came out of the interview room feeling worse than ever. It was his fourth interview in a row. He had deposited at least a hundred resume to every office he could apply in response to advertisements as also unsolicited.

The usual questions at the interview perplexed him.

'How much experience do you have?'

'What is your future plan?'

'Why do you want to do this job?'

Such a series of questions from senseless interviewers appalled him greatly. Really, you are expecting experience from a freshly passed out Postgraduate? If you do not give him the job where the hell is he going to get that experience? And what plans will he make in an empty pocket? And, why would people want a job - isn't that quite obvious? When these questions were again thrown at him today, Pushpendu was tempted to return the very question to his interviewer. Why do *you* want to do this job? Of course, he couldn't retort with such a cheeky response. He went out of the interview room fuming with humiliation.

If they can't provide you with the job you require why do these morons have to offend you? What right do they have to make all those snide remarks? To taunt and torture young men and women who are just searching a way to earn their bread. And to cap it all the salaries offered at private offices in Kolkata is a joke. That too a big one! Then why do the employers seem to have an attitude when they are not even capable to offer a suitable remuneration?

HONK!

Pushpendu jumped back to the pavement cursing the driver. Thinking about employers and this unfair world he was almost going to be hit by a rushing car.

Heart beating fast, he stood still for an instant before crossing the road. Instead of going home he slid past the gates of Deshapriya Park and slumped on a bench. Pushpendu was only 23 but burdened with a lot of expectations on his young shoulders. At home, he had a retired father, an ailing mother and a young, unmarried sister.

The prevailing darkness was slowly removing the last rays of the setting sun. Pushpendu ignored the grumble of his empty stomach and lit a cigar.

He was absorbed in ceaseless, no use thoughts when a man took the seat beside him. Pushpendu hesitated and threw the cigar in a trash-can beside him.

The man approvingly said, 'That's nice of you!'

Pushpendu did not know what to reply as he was not used to receiving appreciation. He was unsuccessful but not impolite.

The man now looked at him and asked, 'Coming from an interview?'

Pushpendu was startled. How would this man know that! As if the man read his mind and said, 'You're carrying your certificates in that see-through folder, you're dressed neatly in office attire … but of course, you're *not* an office employee or how would you sit on the park bench at this time?' The man chuckled. 'So, I understood you must be coming from an interview!'

Pushpendu was still recovering from his bad mood and did not show any reaction to this incredible prediction. Instead, he observed the man now. He was in his mid-forties, hair thinning from the front of his head and a round paunch protruded out of a colourful Tee. He wore a pair of faded denim, a cheap sunglass was poking out from his front pocket. The man was still smiling at him revealing his mismatched teeth.

'The interview went bad, right?' the man asked.

Pushpendu got up. He was not in a mood to discuss his interview with strangers. Such questions were already waiting for him as soon as he would reach home.

'Oh, you got hurt! I didn't mean to.' Said the man patting on the bench. 'Please sit back, young man!'

Pushpendu hesitatingly sat back. He did not want to reach home this early and there was no other place around where he could sit without paying a price.

'No more questions about the interview then,' the man declared. 'What's your aim young fellow?'

'Well, to find a job,' replied Pushpendu dully.

'Job ain't an aim, brother!' The man tore open a plastic packet of peanuts and offered to Pushpendu.

'No, thanks!'

'Take some,' the man insisted. 'You must be hungry!'

Pushpendu never ate food offered by a stranger. Isn't it the first warning you get as a child from your parents? But he took some nuts and put it into his mouth. The man also took a mouthful and started chewing noisily.

This man had asked him a question the answer to which Pushpendu probably wrote in an English essay at school. It seemed like a distant past and whatever he wrote he could not remember now. He was sorry to see the man was still watching him intently.

'Don't mind me saying this but you are depressed and do you know why you're depressed? Because you don't have an aim!'

'What? Of course, I am a bit worried about my career but I do have an ambition …'

'Really? What's your ambition? We don't even know each other! You can share your secret with me.' The man's eyes twinkled.

Pushpendu was impressed that a stranger speculated about he being depressed and this man was interested in his ambition when his own father never bothered himself with such woes.

He cleared his throat and said, 'Well, I want to grab a high-paying job, earn good money and … have a grand life!'

The man stared at him for a while and then at his own feet unmindfully. 'You don't get it,' he shook his head disapprovingly. 'You're doing the same mistake most young people do after college.'

'What's the mistake in that?' Pushpendu said, with a baffled look on his face.

'Chasing money, not knowing what your calling is—'

'So, according to you chasing money is bad?'

'Yes, of course!'

Pushpendu fell silent. When you have no earning member in your family, chasing money whether good or bad, is quite essential, he thought.

The stranger was quiet too but then he continued again. 'See, money is important. You need it to quiet the pangs of your hunger and you need it for every little thing in this world but chasing money doesn't help! It never comes that way …'

Pushpendu was nettled. 'How does it come then?'

'By chasing your dreams! You find out what's your cup of tea and the tea will come along with the cup that is to say, the money will come along if you do your *thing*, you see!' the man said knowingly.

Pushpendu was now considering the stranger with more respect. Of course, this man raised a very important question in his mind. 'What do you do, Sir?'

'Difficult to explain,' the man smiled. 'Let's say, I counsel young people like you.'

'Oh, so you are a counsellor then!' Pushpendu was thrilled. The day was not a complete waste after all! 'But … how do I find what's my cup of tea?'

'Start thinking! Think of the things you used to do happily as a child … things that you did really well and forgot the time while doing it …'

'I don't remember any such thing,' Pushpendu said immediately.

'You have to think deeply. Close your eyes and think now!'

'What? Now?'

'Yes! NOW!'

It was evening and the sky was now dark with the many dazzling stars in it. Crickets were buzzing from the nearby bushes. Men and women were coming in and out of the park, sitting on benches, most of them occupied in their cell phones. Pushpendu and this man were in a corner and nobody really noticed them. Pushpendu closed his eyes.

The man started instructing him. 'Focus now on your childhood. What was something you loved to do? Concentrate your mind. Think … think on.'

Pushpendu concentrated but nothing came into his mind. The sound of the crickets grew noisier, distant voices became clearer but he could not get the answer he was looking for. After some time he opened his eyes with exasperation. The man was staring at the fences and shaking his feet moodily.

'I didn't get to know!' said Pushpendu frustratingly.

'What did you expect? You will close your eyes and get the answer instantly!'

'Isn't that what you said?'

'This is an exercise I just taught you,' said the man wisely. 'You've never thought about your calling … have you? You've just started thinking now. Do it again and again! The answer will come, I'm sure.'

'Really?'

'Yes, of course! The answer comes if asked - you still have time - the later you ask this question the difficult it is to get the answer,' the man heaved a sigh and got up. 'Goodbye young man! I need to go now.'

'Oh, I need to go too. It's past seven! Between … my name is Pushpendu Ghatak. What's your name, Sir?'

'What's in a name?' The man laughed dramatically. 'Recall me as the nameless man who you met on a park bench!' And then with a pat on his back, the man disappeared.

Pushpendu returned home and was confronted with the usual queries by his father, the same accusations that he was not serious enough, and so on. But it did not affect him tonight. Smiling to himself, he went to his room. He will have to think on his cup of tea.

That's an important question nobody asked him before. Not his parents not even his teachers. He changed his shirt and then it dawned. His small leather wallet was missing. He checked his trouser pockets but no it was not there either! Was it when he closed his eyes on the park bench that the man...?

Pushpendu grinned.

There were two hundred rupees and some loose change in the wallet. It was a very small price to pay. He will always remember that man. He will remain in his memory about the nameless man on the park bench who asked him the question others had failed to ask.

———◦◦◦———

THE CAKE SHOP

Manotosh Chatterjee glanced at the shop's display and sighed. The chocolate laden pastries, doll-like cupcakes and a whole world of creamy, delightful things were neatly arranged in racks he had never seen in his life. And the names of these heavenly delicacies were also eye-catching - Chocolate lollypops, Die for Chocolate, Love at first sight, Don't leave me alone, Chocolate delights, and so on.

'Will you like to have anything, Sir?' An assistant half-opened the door and peered at the old gentleman with a courteous smile. The cool air from the insides came rushing out and touched the face of the balded gentleman.

'Not right now, thanks!' Mr Chatterjee piped up in a rather embarrassing tone. The assistant went inside.

This was not the first time Mr Chatterjee stood at the display of the cake shop. On his way to his daily grocery shopping, he would often stand behind the glass window loaded with pastries. He never stepped inside; the price tags attached to those delicacies have warned him to walk into the shop. For a retired old man living on the interests of his small savings of a lifetime, it was rather a fanciful idea to buy expensive cakes.

The cake shop had just opened a few weeks back. It dazzled like a dream in the middle-class locality. And Mr Chatterjee, who was a calm old gentleman with little or no expectations from life, could not resist this urge to stop by the shop and stare longingly at the pretty-looking pastries. It has become more of a childish fascination for him. He and his wife stayed in his ancestral house in Kasba. They had a roof-top, money to live by and their only son married and well-off. Life, as it seemed although not showered a lot of blessings on him, had in a way provided him with the bare essentials. And he had never complained about life.

But this new cake shop that stood on the way to his daily errands had created new hopes in his mind. He wanted to buy some pastries for his wife from this shop. His wife had given her heart and soul to build their nest, to raise their son and Mr Chatterjee nowadays reflected on how little he had given her in return.

He remembered how Somlata had once looked longingly at a saree in a shop display at Gariahat many summers back. It was a peacock blue saree and would have really suited her well. But Biltu's school fee got increased, house repairs were to be done and the budget was really tight. Somlata did not request her husband to buy that saree for her. Still, Manotosh promised his wife he would buy her the saree later on. But he did not or rather could not.

There were always more bills to be paid, things to buy, urgent situations to be met and Biltu's educational expenses only got increased every year. Several years passed and Manotosh never managed an extra ten thousand to buy the saree. He knew the saree had long been bought by some rich lady and even so he could not forget the brilliant peacock blue shade of the silk saree.

In his solitude, Manotosh Babu often remembered the saree and wished if he could have bought it for Somlata. Such is middle-class life, you have a lot of dreams and you hold them so close to your heart not even realizing when none of that happens in reality.

A new fascination had taken hold of Manotosh Babu. He wanted to bring home some of the cakes from the new cake shop. The cakes were a few hundred apiece, as he had peeped from the shop window. Money was indeed limited for him and if he brought those cakes suddenly at home, Somlata might even scold him for the extravagancy.

On his way home, Manotosh Chatterjee reflected on the matter and then it occurred to him. Next week it was their marriage anniversary. What if he bought some beautiful looking pastries for his wife on that occasion? She will hardly reprove him. Maybe she will laugh at her husband's childishness? After retirement Manotosh Babu was not able to give her a piece of fine jewellery or buy anything expensive. Last year he was even saving money for a vacation, but all the money got used in house repairs.

This year Somlata said to her husband any money that could be saved would be put aside in case of an emergency. In old age, there was no dearth of emergencies.

'No need to waste money on unnecessary things,' she said.

'Vacation does not come under unnecessary things!' Manotosh Babu had argued. 'We need a break! Over ten years we haven't gone anywhere except if you count the trip to Digha which I certainly do not count!'

Manotosh Chatterjee made a decision. He had never bought anything expensive for himself or his wife ever and this anniversary he was finally going to give a little taste of luxury to his wife.

Reaching home Manotosh Babu entered the bathroom singing his favourite Shyama Sangeet, '*Maa go anandomoyee niranando koro naa ...*'

Manotosh Chatterjee had planned it all. He will do some cost-cutting here and there and will buy those lovely looking cakes for his wife. He was quite in gay spirits and when Somlata asked him the reason he just chuckled. 'Madam, who said an old man can't be happy?'

Finally the day before their anniversary date, Manotosh Babu slipped out of his house in the evening and went to the cake shop. He stepped inside the shop proudly. The interiors of the shop which had dazzled in front of him like a distant dream was finally within his reach. It's not such a big deal, after all, thought Mr Chatterjee. You might as well catch some of your dreams in this life!

He chose some of those chocolate stuffed soft pastries. Somlata loved chocolates so much. Taste does not change with age. Does it? And then he chose some of those doll shaped cupcakes. Their son and daughter-in-law will also join them the next evening. Somlata would be happy to give a nice tea party to them, he thought. When the bill was produced, his heart trembled a little. Two thousand and some more. The price was not much, Manotosh Babu reasoned if it could bring a smile to his wife's face.

While returning he also bought a bouquet of fresh red roses from the roadside stall. His wife had gone to their neighbour's place and he used this time well. It was the month of January and he did not have to keep the box of cakes in the fridge. Instead, he hid the box in his cupboard and placed the bouquet behind the newspaper rack. After keeping the things he congratulated himself for this intelligent planning. The next morning he would present the box of cakes and flowers to his wife.

Manotosh Babu was eager to see his wife's reaction. It seemed to him that the night was too long.

The next morning he arranged the box of cakes and the bouquet on the kitchen table. Somlata would find it the first thing in the morning after entering the kitchen to prepare the breakfast. Satisfied with the arrangement, he went out for his usual stroll.

Manotosh Babu started walking briskly and then his steps slowed down unexpectedly. He started breathing heavily while his heart pounded hastily. Was it the excitement or the weather? He half-completed the walk and started to return. He was just near his building when his eyes started to blur, his head became dizzy and heart raced faster until he was engulfed in darkness. He fell on the hard pavement and could not remember anymore.

When he opened his eyes he found himself lying in a hospital bed surrounded by white walls and a variety of strange machines that beeped and buzzed, their lights piercing his eyes. His hands have been channelled and bottles of saline and other liquids were hanging around his bed. Manotosh babu tried to lift his head when an unknown female voice from the back warned him. 'Stay like that! Don't you move, Sir.'

He fell into a stupor. He reopened his eyes to see his wife and son watching him intently.

'When have you come? What has happened to me?'

His wife gestured him to stay calm while his son informed he had a heart attack and the doctor had suggested surgery to place a pacemaker.

'It's lucky you fell on the pavement and not on the main road,' Somlata sniffed. 'Don't worry, we will take you back home.'

After his wife and son were gone, Manotosh Babu reflected on how he had planned to surprise his wife today. Somlata was indeed surprised but this was not how he had intended to.

Returning home Somlata calculated their fixed deposits. Biltu had agreed to pay one lakh for the surgery and she would arrange the remaining money from their bank deposits.

The next morning Biltu and his wife waited in their car for Somlata. She just reached the car and then stopped.

'Maa, what are you waiting for? asked Biltu.

'I have forgotten my phone, please wait for me a little, I'll just go and …'

'Maa, you get in, give me the keys, I'll just rush and bring it!' said her daughter-in-law.

'Thank you, Bou-maa. It's on the kitchen table.'

Somlata waited inside the car while her daughter-in-law went upstairs. She took a while and returned with an odd expression on her face.

'Maa, can I ask you something?'

'Yes, what?'

'Baba always says that he has to live on his little savings …'

'Yes, because that's true!' replied Somlata in a tone of surprise. It was an odd time to discuss such matters.

'What's this about?' demanded Biltu from the driver's seat.

His wife now turned to him and said, 'I just found a box of cakes in your mother's kitchen. It's from that new cake shop,' she informed while getting into the car. 'The one we bought cakes from last Sunday.'

'And so?'

'Those are really expensive ones!' his wife retorted. 'Particularly for a retired man to buy from that shop means …'

'Means what?' Somlata asked her daughter-in-law from the backseat with a look of disbelief in her eyes.

'Maa, it just means the box of cakes must have cost at least a thousand! So, do you have enough money to keep wasting like that?'

'Enough!' said Somlata.

'Why Maa? Why are you getting so annoyed?' asked Biltu starting the car. 'She didn't say anything wrong! Those cakes are really expensive. Besides those are full of cream and sugar and all rich stuff ... I don't think you should have them at all!'

'That's what I wanted to say,' remarked his wife. 'Not good for your pockets, not good for your health! Don't mind me saying this, but I s'pose Baba had fallen ill for those cakes.'

The whole discussion was sickening for Somlata. She did not want to argue back and quietly wiped her eyes. When the car took a turn she caught a glimpse of the glossy doors of the new cake shop.

THE RICKSHAW

PULLER

Ronit looked at the sky. It was lightning from time to time. Grabbing two big bags full of monthly groceries he crossed the crowded street and desperately looked for a rickshaw. It would rain anytime. The fastest way to return home was to take a rickshaw, of course, if he was fortunate enough to get one. In the locality of Gariahat, nowadays the hand-drawn rickshaws are almost becoming a rare sight.

At this hour of need, Ronit deeply reflected on why these rickshaws were so less in the city. Were the rickshaw pullers changing their trades? But why? It never occurred to him before. Maybe when you are in need of something only then you start to think about it. He walked on the pavement carefully avoiding the street vendors and their enthusiastic customers. It's a difficult job to walk on the pavements of Gariahat particularly when your hands are full.

Just as he turned towards a by-lane he was relieved to see an old rickshaw puller waiting alone. Ronit rushed to him, thrust his bags to the old man and got up. He lived in Purna Das Road which was only a small walk away but with two heavy bags and an inevitable rain, the rickshaw was indeed a life-saver now. He took back his bags and sat somewhat uncomfortably. The rickshaw started moving.

The rickshaw went noisily through the lanes, tinkling its bell and shaking its passenger as the wheels dragged through the black pitched road. The rickshaw puller took speed while coughing and shivering a little in the wintery evening air. Ronit wanted to cover his face. He heard these poor old folks often had untreated tuberculosis.

Having clutched his bags he was unable to protect himself from the germs and so there was a revolted look on Ronit's face.

After many more minutes when Ronit finally reached home he was extremely pleased.

'Koto debo?' he asked the man his fare.

'Teesh rupay dijiye babu.' The old man said it was thirty rupees.

'Ki bolcho ki! Teesh rupay! Bollei holo naki? Ami e parar lok. Ei tuku hoy naki tirish taka?' Ronit was agitated the little ride cost him this much. From his pocket, he took out a twenty rupees note and handed to the man.

The man refused. Unwillingly and cursing under his breath, Ronit took out another ten rupees note and gave it to the man.

The rickshaw puller now took the money and drove away. While Ronit waited on his door he heard the rattling of the rickshaw and the coughs of the man at a distance.

His wife helped him with the bags after opening the door. She could see a look of annoyance on her husband's face.

'What happened?' she asked. 'You look a little irritated.'

'Don't ask! The rickshaw man was a thief. He charged thirty rupees from Gariahat.'

'What?'

'And all the way, he coughed and coughed. Don't know if he was a TB patient …'

'Oh, no! Please take a bath and I'll wash your clothes right now!'

It started raining when Ronit went to the bathroom. And when he opened his clothes to give those to his wife for washing, he realized it. He did not have his purse.

No, no, no ... it can't be! Ronit changed quickly and rushed out of the bathroom. He looked on the doorway and then ran into the deserted road where the rickshaw had stopped a while ago. There was no sign of his purse anywhere.

If the purse had dropped on the road could anyone take it by this time? That would have been possible but the weather was foul and there was not a single person or even an animal around. People usually do not hang around in the winter rain.

Ronit entered the house in soaked clothes and a deep frown on his forehead. He looked around hopelessly.

His wife looked at him with a perturbed expression on her face. 'Why did you go out in the rain?'

Ronit stared at his wife unable to speak any word.

'What's happened? Will you please tell me?'

The initial shock being over Ronit said what had just happened.

'But you paid the man from your purse, right?'

'No, I paid from the loose change in my pocket.'

'What if you dropped your purse in this dealing and the man watched it. As you've turned he'd silently picked it up …'

'Yes …yes …it must be! What should I do now?'

'Block all your cards! Immediately! And then let's go to the place where you got the rickshaw. Maybe we'll just catch him there …'

'He won't be there waiting for us now! What're you talking about? Even if you find him he's not going to admit, will he? I am blocking my cards, that's all!'

'How much cash was there?'

'Ten thousand and some more … drawn from the ATM this evening … forget it!'

'What? Won't you complain to the police?'

'I said forget it,' Ronit said firmly and went to his room.

The following week Ronit was so busy at the office he almost forgot his breakfasts. This was in one way good for him as he did not get much time to brood on the lost wallet. At times when he recalled that particular evening and the rickshaw puller, he immediately felt a jolt in the pit of his stomach.

In a quiet cold Sunday morning when Ronit was having tea in his living room, there was a loud knock on the door.

'Now, who's that on this hour?' Exasperated, he went to answer the door.

As he opened the door he was surprised to see the visitor. It was the old rickshaw wala, wearing his tattered vest and a folded lungi, looking shabbier in the daylight. The man smiled at Ronit showing his yellow, uneven teeth. Before he could be asked a question, the old man extended his hand and produced the brown purse Ronit lost two weeks back.

Stunned, Ronit stared at the wallet and then at the man before taking it back.

'Apka purse gir gaya tha saab, mera ricksha mein … jab hum dekhe tab hum laut gaye they… phir lautane ke liye aa nahi paye, bahut bimaar ho gaya tha … aj thoda thik huye to ake de diye saab. Dekh lijiye babu apka purse jaisa tha waisa hi hai!'

Ronit opened his wallet. All the notes of five hundred were neatly placed exactly the way he had arranged those after withdrawing from the ATM that evening. The old man now turned and Ronit looked at his thin slippers. It was a chilly morning and the man shivered a little. Today he did not bring his rickshaw.

'Ricksha wala dada, thoda rukiye na …'

The man stopped. Ronit rushed to him and taking out a five hundred rupees note from his purse handed to the old man.

The rickshaw puller looked at Ronit for a moment, grinned and then turned away the hand and the note.

'Apka purse apko lautaya … isme kya hain? … inaam nahi chahiye saab, hum garib admi hain per hum mehnet karke kama lete hain saab!' And the man turned away, walking slowly.

Ronit stood blankly on the sidewalk clutching the five hundred rupees note. He could hear the old rickshaw puller's coughs fading at a distance.

HAIRCUT

O n a hot afternoon, inside an old-fashioned apartment in Dhakuria, Saheli Sengupta stands at the tall mirror of her dressing table, untangling knee-length hair with her fingers. An old Bollywood song comes floating in the air through her half-opened window. She observes her dark black hair with mild admiration.

Saheli is not pretty, far from that but her hair is her glory and pride. When she lets her hair open, people never fail to notice her black dense beauty – ever! Her hair is like black satin and as dark as the night sky.

Her husband even chose her, awe-admired with her hair. She was standing at the Radha-Krishna temple wearing her mother's saree when Subir noticed her for the first time from the back. He saw the long, wavy hair and pieces of sunlight dazzling in her hair like the many stars in the black sky.

At 36, Saheli has quite a busy schedule – at home. From the morning tea to arranging lunch boxes for her children and husband, tidying her house, she has no time to pause, let alone rest. Afternoons are her only time to herself.

She does not like to take afternoon naps like the other housewives. She reads books or simply sits and observes life beyond her window.

Saheli often witnesses scenes from life that otherwise is unobserved by the world. Tired salesmen, sweating and walking hopelessly on the streets, man and woman fighting on the road, a college girl sitting on the doorsteps of Mr Gupta and crying her eyes out and today she just overheard a man talking over his mobile phone probably blackmailing someone.

Saheli watches things, drawing conclusions in her mind, sometimes worrying for complete strangers and sometimes unperturbed by whatsoever happened in the world beyond her bedroom window. She often imagines herself in a safe bubble and on the other side of that bubble is another world, where people are playing roles and Saheli is a witness to parts of their plays.

She takes out her old 'Sanchaita' from the bookshelf when her mother-in-law enters the room. 'Have you not asked Rupali to cook the dinner before leaving? She won't be coming this evening, do you remember?'

'Oh, yes, I know that Maa. Her son is ill. So, I didn't feel like asking her anything … don't worry … I'll manage it all.'

'Very well, then! Today Piu is coming for dinner! I'd told you, remember?'

'Did you?' said Saheli in a low voice more to herself than to her mother-in-law. Piu is her nanad, her husband's only sister. And if she is coming she must be coming with her husband and two children. Piu is a perfectionist and she expects everything to be prim and proper – always.

'Er … okay … don't worry … I'll manage everything!' Saheli says in a convincing tone and her mother-in-law walks out of the room.

Saheli now ties her hair and goes to the kitchen. If Piu is coming she should start the preparations now.

Dinner is a sumptuous affair with fried rice, chicken gravy, fish chops, chicken legs, salads, rasogollas and fruit custard. Saheli keeps on insisting second helpings to everyone. Piu, who dislikes talking while on the dinner table, just observes and remarks nothing.

When dinner is finally over, the children start playing and running in and out of rooms, Subir takes his brother-in-law to their spacious living room and the ladies shifts to Saheli's bedroom.

Piu slouches lazily in her sister-in-law's bed and suddenly remarks, 'Boudi don't you trim your hair?'

Saheli smiles and replies she never gets the time to go to a salon besides she loves her hair long.

'Don't get the time? What do you mean, Boudi?' says Piu. 'Are you really that busy? I mean … I've got a job, two kids at home … and I still get time for the salon once or twice a month!'

Piu has a full-time help and her mother-in-law manages the household whenever she isn't around but Saheli is unable to point that out to her sister-in-law.

'What she means is,' says Saheli's mother-in-law, without taking her eyes from the magazine she is browsing, '*I* do not let her have any time to herself.'

'No … I didn't mean that,' objects Saheli but her mother-in-law gestures her to stop.

Piu now looks at Saheli with an odd expression on her face. 'But Boudi you can still trim your hair sometimes, the ends are not looking nice at all! If you say, I can do it for you!'

'No, I – I really don't need anything. But thanks for offering the help though!'

'What Boudi! You're not smart at all, if you don't mind me saying this! Women of your age nowadays look like they go to college and you …'

Saheli tries to change the topic without offending her sister-in-law but Piu is quite stubborn. If Piu has her mind on something she will keep on pushing until you surrender to her.

'I do not like your hair at all! And it's really the only thing that's quite nice about you - don't mind - but I like speaking the truth!' Piu says in a matter-of-fact tone.

'I know,' admits Saheli, 'there's nothing to mind, but I don't want to experiment with my hair…'

'Oh, who says to experiment with your hair? No, Boudi, let me just help you! I promise your hair will only look better after a trim.'

Saheli looks at her mother-in-law for support but she finds her deeply absorbed in the magazine.

'Look, I'll send my hair-dresser. You won't have to go anywhere, she'll just give a little touch on your hair. That's it!'

Two mornings later, a hairdresser truly appears at Saheli's doorsteps. 'Ma'am, I was booked for a haircut schedule at your place. Is it for you?'

'Er ... yes ... please come in!'

Nobody is at home today; even her mother-in-law has gone to the temple. Saheli takes the woman to the living room and asks her to take a seat while she goes to her room and nervously starts pacing near the window.

She glances through the window and suddenly observes something she never quite noticed before. Housewives heaving their children to school, office-going women walking past hurriedly and even elderly ladies out for their usual grocery shopping – none of them has long hair! Of course, they are the women of the metro city and look like that. If Saheli stands with them she would indeed look odd. Some of these ladies have really short hair but most of them have medium length hair, fashionably cut and styled.

Saheli had never cut her hair; in fact, she had never gone to a salon. Her hair is gorgeous as everyone remarks but she never paid much attention to it. She returns to the living room and asks the hairdresser what hairstyle would suit her.

After the haircut is done, the hairdresser woman returns happily with some extra tip and Saheli returns to her dressing table to observe her hair from every angle. Heart thumping she realizes she looks different now and remembers the remark given to her by the hairdresser, 'You look absolutely stunning!' Saheli's hair now ends to her shoulders with beautiful fringes on both sides.

She imagines what Subir will say when he sees her in a completely new look and smiles. What was Piu telling the other day? *Women of her age look like college girls.* Saheli admires her haircut one more time. *Well, so much with hair. I look so young now!*

It turns out things do not happen as Saheli imagined. An hour later her mother-in-law returns with a friend and looks at Saheli with an expression of someone who had seen a ghost in the broad daylight.

'What have you done with your hair?' her mother-in-law remarks, 'you look terrible!'

Her friend supports her in this. 'Saheli, your hair was the only beauty you had! What did you cut it for?'

Saheli rushes to her room, locks herself and stands at the mirror, this time tears streaming her eyes and the blurred reflection shakes uncontrollably in front of her. *What have I done? I have lost the only beauty I had!*

In the evening when Subir returns from office, his mother comes to him immediately and remarks, 'Go and see your wife …'

'Why? What happened?' asks Subir in a tired voice.

'She didn't have lunch. Must be crying her eyes out —'

'What for? Have you said something?'

'I knew it! You'll put the blame on me even before knowing anything!'

'Oh, Maa, then tell me, what has happened?'

'She has done a haircut - all her hair's gone and she can't come out of her room.'

Subir goes to their room and finds Saheli sitting in the corner of the bed, looking outside the window. He comes in front of her, removes the pallu that was hiding her back and says shockingly, 'Oh, you really have cut all your hair!'

'How do I look?'

'Not good,' says Subir disapprovingly. 'You could've asked me once before doing this stupid haircut!'

'Mom, you look absolutely pretty!' says a voice from the back. Their daughter, Titli has just returned home from her tuitions.

'Really, your Mom shouldn't have cut her hair!' insists Subir. 'But what's done is done! Ask her to come out of the room.'

'Papa, please. She looks lovely!' Titli comes to her mother and sits beside her. 'You look gorgeous, Mrs Sengupta! I didn't like your long hair much!'

'Really?' asks Saheli smiling faintly.

Saheli's mother-in-law enters the room looking sombre as if someone had died. 'Titli, stop false praising your mother. She should understand what mistake she's done!'

'Oh, she hasn't made a mistake! Women of her age do not keep such long hairs like you lot!' says Titli.

'Keep out of this Titli, you don't understand,' replies her grandmother and then turns to Saheli and says, 'I told everything to Piu and she's feeling so bad! I'd said it's not her fault but yours! She asked you to trim but you'd cut it short!'

After a few moments of silence, Saheli starts laughing. Her husband and mother-in-law exchanges nervous glances.

When the fit of laughter subsides, Saheli replies, 'Please tell Piu, thanks for sending the hairdresser and *not* to feel bad for me.'

Her mother-in-law starts, 'But …'

Saheli gestures her to stop. 'It's *my* hair, you see! I'm to decide what to do with it.' Saheli now gets up from her bed and says, 'I'm going to fix some pasta. Who's hungry?'

'Me, me, me!' says Tili dancing around her mother. They leave the room and Subir stares at his mother whose mouth is half-open wearing a shocked expression.

DECEMBER RAINS

I t was a usual day for Riddhima until then. But now the unusual thing happened she could no longer enlist this Friday in the calendar just like any other mundane day. Not anymore.

The day was going on exactly as it should. Her arrogant boss screamed at her without a reason, Mrs Sen was as usual mean, Roy Babu as nosy as ever, the office food was as usual tasteless, the never-ending files, complaining co-workers all behaved exactly as they should. In fact, the long wait for the returning auto was also the same. Only then something happened that changed the flavour of the entire day for Riddhima.

A small five minutes unexpected conversation completely changed her mood. The people on the streets now appeared merrier, the noisy children looked like angels and even the stuffy auto seemed to be more comfortable to Riddhima. Kolkata is quite chilly in December. As she stepped out of the auto it started to drizzle. The cold droplets touched her bare face and hands bringing a shiver in her backbone.

The damp weather could not, however, dampen the spirit of Riddhima. While standing on the Sovabazar metro station and waiting for her train, Riddhima was smiling in spite of her. This was a rare scene indeed because people who knew her had forgotten how she smiled. In fact, Riddhima has obviously forgotten how to work her facial muscles anymore. Her fellow passengers on the train might not have noticed this unusual thing because their eyes were glued to their mobile screens. But there was a definite change in her expressions.

Someone who has noticed Riddhima all these years would vouch there was definitely an unexciting and extremely serious thing about her. The air around her smelled nothing but of seriousness. Her colleagues even called her 'boring Riddhi' at her back. This evening, tired though she was like any other day returning home she was positively blushing.

Before going into the detail of how this quiet, reserved lady suddenly changed her aura, allow me to give you a sincere account on her life story. Riddhima Bose is of 36 years, had never married and evidently, she had ruled out the option of it from her life. Riddhima is highly educated, decent looking and does a not-so-bad job in Salt Lake area. Her father died when she was quite young and now she lives with her mother in their ancestral house in Nandi Street.

What most people do not know is that she had fallen in love once in her life. It was not a fairytale romance although Riddhima placed a lot of high hopes in that relationship. She was in college then and like many other romances, her love story was over with college. After that Riddhima failed to believe in the concept of love. Her mother insisted a lot many times about marriage but it never stirred her up. Actually, she was way too serious for people to understand her.

You see, the world does not function that way. Here people change their decisions and break their promises every now and then. Riddhima being so serious had taken her relationship so seriously that she could not believe in all seriousness her boyfriend could leave her. He did leave her anyway. Only Riddhima could not move on.

Life went on but her heart stayed frozen. Riddhima was not waiting for her ex. Maybe she was trying to make the time stop. But there she was wrong. Time flew faster than she thought. She did not realize how the years passed after college. All the years that came and went, each and every day of these sixteen years were almost the same. For her.

This evening while waiting for the auto something very different happened with Riddhima for the first time in many years. A man about her age appeared out of nowhere and asked, 'Riddhi?'

Overcoming the surprise, she had replied, 'Yes? Do I know you?'

'So, you couldn't recognize me?' The stranger laughed heartily. 'It's expected though!'

The man had sharp features concealed in well-groomed beard and moustache. He had deep brown eyes if anyone looked at them beyond his glasses. His breath smelled of freshly taken cigar and he had a familiar smile.

Riddhima stared for a moment before exclaiming, 'Arijit! Yes, isn't it?'

The clean-shaven boyish face had totally changed, so has his built. In college days he appeared as lanky but now he looked confident with well-built arms and a sturdy frame.

'You look exactly the same,' said Arijit. 'Only the hair… it's shorter now.'

Riddhima had beautiful, waist-length hair in college days. It was her pride back then.

The two friends were delighted to see each other after so many years. It seemed like it was only yesterday they went to college. Arijit Dutta was a good friend of Riddhima. After college, he had gone abroad for higher studies and Riddima started working to support her family.

Nowadays distance did not mean anything because of the internet but Riddhima made sure she was not to be found. After the break-up she internalized the concept of life. To her life was a struggle and she was doing that part quite sincerely. She had purposely detached herself from friends.

'Riddhi, why aren't you on Facebook?' Arijit said in a complaining tone. 'This is so bad! I mean I tried to contact you …'

'Well, I don't have an exciting life that's why am not there,' Riddhima said indifferently.

There was sarcasm in her voice which her old friend easily understood. He changed the topic and said, 'Can I at least get your number?'

Arijit returned to Kolkata a year back. He had started a consultancy company. The incredible thing was that his office was just opposite Riddhima's office building. Only they never met until today. This evening Arijit had come to Ultadanga to meet a friend and suddenly noticed Riddhima standing on the queue for auto. Instantly he recognized her because she looked almost the same.

The two friends exchanged their numbers before Riddhima got her auto.

This small conversation changed the tone of the day for her. She suddenly remembered her good old college days and started to feel wistful. Gone were those days but there were so many bitter-sweet memories. This evening she realized she had hidden all her memories in a secret chamber of her heart. She had buried so many beautiful moments of college life deep inside to forget the hurt she received as a young girl.

To Riddhima, the past college days was synonymous to her failed love life that she did not want to recall at all. Over the years she has become like a robot. She woke up every day to go to the office and then return every night to go to the office the next morning. Her work has become her life. Meeting Arijit after all this time suddenly made her realize that she was not yet forgotten. She still was remembered by a friend.

Every day after returning from the office she takes a bath, eats dinner silently and then shuts herself in her room. She reads till the time she falls asleep. Then another day starts with the preparation of going to the office and it ends with her returning home.

This evening for the first time she noticed their neighbour's five-year-old daughter from the balcony. 'She is such a sweetheart,' Riddhima remarked to her mother.

At night she did not lock herself in the room. She watched TV with her mother and then sang one of her mother's favourite Rabindra Sangeet. She could sing really well, only she did not pursue it after college. Riddhima abandoned everything after college that was close to her. Except of course her mother and the love for books.

The next morning Riddhima received a text from Arijit.'What's your lunchtime at the office? Let's meet at the *Chai Break*!'

Today Riddhima gave attention to her appearance. She shampooed her hair, wore a pale lip colour and there was also a hint of kajal in her eyes. Before going to the office she checked her reflection twice.

Why am I even doing this? Enquired a small voice. A second voice replied this is just necessary. *I can't go out for lunch looking like a zombie!*

Riddhima could not remember when was the last time she met a friend. She never met anyone, for the matter. She never went anywhere other than her office. As she was on the way again a small voice popped in her head. *So, is it kind of a date? You very well know that Arijit had a feeling for you! What? No! He's just my friend! Maybe he's even got married!*

At college, Arijit was her secret admirer. He never expressed his feelings to his best friend's girlfriend. But Riddhima, like any other woman, sensed his affection for her. Arijit never revealed his love for Riddhima and she never expressed that she did realize his feelings for her.

Arijit Dutta was waiting inside the restaurant. Riddhima pushed the door mildly and entered like a fresh breeze. Wearing a yellow salwar suit, hair pulled back, she was looking like a woman in her early twenties. Arijit rose from his seat with a broad smile. 'Finally! Finally, we meet, after all!'

'Yes!' said Riddhima smilingly.

Arijit glanced at her as if he wanted to say something and then stopped. Instead, he fidgeted with the salt tray moodily.

'How's your business doing?' asked Riddhima.

'My business? Yeah, going great! Thanks.'

Both of them fell silent for some time. Riddhima was embarrassed to find heat rising in her cheeks. She wanted the conversation to get going but Arijit was not helping.

When the food arrived Arijit started arranging the plates and asked, 'What's new?'

'Nothing at all!' answered Ridhhima. 'Same story, every day. Office and home.'

'Why don't you try something new then?' Arijit insisted.

'Well, I don't have time after office, you see!'

'Can't you change your office then?'

'I don't think that's possible!' Riddhima said. 'Let's talk about you. Tell me everything!'

Arijit, of course, had exciting stories to talk about his life at The States and on his new IT venture. Over lunch, Arijit talked a lot. Riddhima mostly listened.

While leaving the restaurant she asked, 'You didn't tell me anything about your wife or girlfriend, maybe?'

Arijit stared at the busy street unmindfully before replying, 'Because I don't have any! What about you?'

'What about me?' Riddhima said. 'I think you know that … that … we broke up … me and Sudhanshu …'

'Yes, I knew it later on,' admitted Arijit. 'And so what? Sudhanshu's got married. He even has a six years old daughter!'

Riddhima did not have this piece of information.

'Sorry, if I'd said something hurtful to you.'

'Oh, no … no … you didn't!

Riddhima was surprised that the news of her ex being married and living happily with his wife and kid did not upset her. In fact, she was not affected at all. Several lonely nights Riddhima imagined if Sudhanshu appeared in front of her as a husband of some other woman how would it make her feel? Now that the news was confirmed by Arijit, she felt no envy or pain rather her heart was lighter than ever.

That night Riddhima slept peacefully without a pill. She woke up late as it was a Sunday and thought of inviting Arijit.

She called him up. 'Hey, Arijit, what's up! What's your plan today?'

'Well, not that I've any plans ...'

'Great! Why don't you come to my place for lunch? Maa will be pleased to see you after all this time!'

'That's really a good idea Riddhi ... but I can't.'

'Why not? Is there a problem?'

'Actually, my parents want me to meet a girl today, you know for —'

'Oh, right! Got it! For getting married.' Riddhima's voice suddenly appeared false and loud.

'Will catch you up later, Riddhi!'

'Bye.'

Riddhima reflected on her life. She never paused to think about whatever happened or did not happen in her life. So, Arijit was getting married. It's not an unusual thing. People get married. Yesterday, while spending time with him she had started feeling nostalgic. All these years she had severed ties with old friends just because she was scared to accept reality.

Riddhima was restless. Her sore heart had just started to heal when this phone call made her realize that she was completely alone. *Why am I even feeling miserable? ... I'd only chosen this life for myself! He disappeared from my life and I didn't even want to find him ... but God knows how much I've missed him all these years! Now that I got him back I thought it would be like old times ... but we are all grown-ups now! He has a life of his own ... he wants to settle down and that's only normal. Oh, God! What have I done with my life?*

Tears started pouring all over her face. She remembered the last time she was heartbroken. She had howled in pain alone in this room. The day Sudhanshu had unexpectedly walked on her. He said it was finished. Only Riddhima could not finish it off. She was left alone by Sudhanshu that day and she is left alone by Arijit today. *Why is life always a struggle for me?*

Riddhima shut her door and switched on the music player. She did not want her mother to know that she was heartbroken for a second time.

Pain is the best teacher if you learn the lesson from it. Riddhima Bose was numb when she was brokenhearted for the first time as a young college girl. This time however after crying her eyes out she started feeling better. In the afternoon she went for a walk by the Ganges. The fresh air rejuvenated her mind.

She remembered a happy childhood memory of walking with her father on the Princep Ghat. Riddhima still felt the touch of her father's hand in hers. Her father had always loved her. Her mother too loves her. Then why has she refused to love herself? All because love was denied to her from the man she desired?

Walking by the Ganges Riddhima realized the true essence of life. Life is not just about getting all the things you want. It's about enjoying each and every moment and staying grateful in your heart.

The next day, at the office everyone looked up at Riddhima Bose as if they were seeing her for the first time. It was partly because she had done a heavy make-up and was wearing a bright orange dress. But the main reason all her colleagues were shocked was that she had submitted a resignation letter to her boss.

This was not a step taken on an emotional surge. Last night she had prepared her mind into doing this. For sixteen years she had mistreated herself which is why she remained in this toxic environment. As if she was punishing herself for not being worthy.

Riddhima now realized that she was worthy. She was worthy enough to work where she would be appreciated. She has the right to choose and from now on she decided to choose only the good for her. The heaviness in her heart she carried over the years having dissolved Riddhima knew exactly what to do.

In the coming weeks, things started to happen exactly the way she intended. Within a week of her resignation, she was selected in a better position in a bigger company. And she joined a music class on Sunday evenings.

One such evening while returning from the class it started to rain. Riddhima ran to a shade. December rains have its charm, observed Riddhima. Her phone buzzed. It was Arijit.

'So, how's life?' demanded Arijit.

'Life's going great actually!' said Riddhima gleefully. And she said all about her new life. Arijit was surprised as also happy for her.

Riddhima remembered their last conversation. 'What happened on that day?' she asked smilingly. 'You didn't tell me anything after that! Any good news?'

Arijit said, 'Well, this sort of meeting with strangers happen once a while. There's nothing to be serious about!'

'What do you mean?' Riddhima asked in a puzzled way.

'Well!' Arijit continued, 'I've to meet these women to please my mother. And then I make some excuse and refuse them.'

'What! Why would you do that, Arijit? It's not fair!'

'I don't want to settle through an arranged marriage… you see … because I …' Arijit paused.

'Because what Arijit? Do you have someone else in your mind?'

'Yes …' replied Arijit hesitatingly.

'Oh, really, so you love someone else?' Riddhima said. 'Why don't you say it to your mother? You'll be saved from this "arranged marriage" drama thing!'

'Hmm … it's not easy dear!'

'Why not?'

'Because I don't know if … if she will accept me!'

'Maybe you should just ask her then.'

'It's difficult Riddima …'

'Of course, it's difficult,' admitted Riddhima.'Does it mean you won't even try? It was difficult for me to change my life. Still, I tried and I did it! Maybe you should also try, Ari.'

'Okay! Well …' Arijit cleared his throat. 'Ridhhi, the woman I've always loved, is YOU! It's you who I wanted to forget all these years but couldn't.' Arijit paused. 'They say marriage is difficult. Would you like to try it with me?'

It had stopped raining. The air was full of a fresh smell of some unknown flower. The clouds have drifted and the sky was clearer. Riddhima started walking.

'Hello, are you still there?'

'Yes!'

'So, what do you think?'

'Well, I'd love to give it a try!'

'Riddhima, you're not joking, right?' Arijit stood up from his couch.

'Of course not, Ari! There was always a deep connection between us. And I always knew you loved me. I really have missed you all these years…'

Grinning ear to ear, Arijit Dutta thumped his fist in the air and jumped.

Made in the USA
Monee, IL
07 July 2026

56551412R00069